DISNEY'S
THE LITTLE
MERMAID

DISNEY'S
Beauty
AND THE
BEAST

WALT DISNEY'S
Cinderella

WALT DISNEY'S
Snow White
and the Seven Dwarfs

Disney
✦ PRINCESS

CD
Storybook

This book belongs to:

KRIST
En

date

CD Storybook

Beauty and the Beast
The Little Mermaid
Cinderella
Snow White

Hinkler Books Pty Ltd 2004
17-23 Redwood Drive
Dingley, VIC, 3172
www.hinklerbooks.com

ISBN 1 8651 5754 6

Printed and manufactured in China.

CD Storybook

Contents

Belle

Once upon a time, a young Prince lived in a shining castle. One cold night an old beggar woman arrived, offering him a single rose in return for shelter. Repulsed by her ugliness, he turned her away. Suddenly, she transformed into a beautiful enchantress.

To punish the Prince, the enchantress cast a spell and turned him into a hideous beast. Then she gave him a magic mirror and an enchanted rose, telling him it would bloom until his twenty-first year. To break the spell, he had to love another and earn that person's love in return, before the last petal fell.

Nearby, in a small village, a beautiful young woman named Belle hurried through town. She rushed to her favorite shop–the bookstore. The owner gave her a book as a gift. A dreamy look crossed Belle's face.

"Far-off places, daring sword fights, magic spells, a prince in disguise ... Oh, thank you very much!"

Belle rushed outside, reading as she walked.

As Belle walked, a handsome hunter named Gaston ran after her.

"Belle, the whole town's talking about you! It's about time you got your nose out of those books."

Then Gaston's friend Le Fou joined them and began to insult her father, an inventor.

"My father's not crazy! He's a genius!" said Belle.

As she spoke, an explosion boomed from her father's cottage.

She quickly ran home.

At the cottage, Belle found her father, Maurice, and told him what the villagers were saying about her. "They think I'm odd, Papa."

"Don't worry, Belle," he said. "My invention is going to change everything for us. We won't have to live in this little town forever!"

Then he hitched up their horse, Phillipe, and set off for the fair with his new invention. Belle waved.

"Good-bye! Good luck!"

But Maurice got lost and accidentally led Phillipe into a bleak, misty forest. Suddenly, he saw two yellow eyes staring out of the darkness. It was a wolf! Phillipe reared, and bolted away. Terrified, Maurice ran through the forest with some wolves racing behind him.

When he reached a tall, heavy gate, Maurice dashed inside.

He slammed it shut on the wolves, who snapped at him with their sharp teeth.

Maurice saw a huge, forbidding castle. Nervously, he walked inside
it. "Hello? I've lost my horse, and I need a place to stay for the night."
"Of course, Monsieur! You are welcome here!" said a voice.
Maurice looked down and saw a mantel clock with a stern, frowning
face. Beside him stood a smiling candelabra! Maurice grabbed the
clock and examined it. "Why—you're alive!" he said.

The enchantress had also turned all the Prince's servants into household objects. As Cogsworth the clock protested, Lumiere, the candelabra, showed Maurice into the drawing room.

Suddenly, the door flew open. A voice boomed.

"There's a stranger here ..."

"Please ... I need a place to stay ..." said Maurice.

"I'll give you a place to stay!" the Beast roared. He grabbed Maurice and dragged him out of the room.

Back home at the cottage, Gaston knocked at the door.

"Gaston! What a 'pleasant' surprise!" said Belle.

"Belle, there's not a girl in town who wouldn't love to be in your shoes. Do you know why? Because I want to marry you!"

"Gaston, I'm speechless! I'm sorry, but ... but ... I just don't deserve you!" said Belle. All the villagers had gathered in Belle's yard, hoping to see a wedding. Gaston was humiliated!

After the villagers and Gaston left, Belle ran outside. There
she found Phillipe, alone. "Phillipe!" she cried. "What are you
doing here?

Where's Papa?"

The horse whinnied anxiously. Frightened, Belle leaped onto
Phillipe and returned to the mysterious forest. Soon, they found
the castle.

"What is this place?" Belle wondered, trying to steady Phillipe.
Then she saw Maurice's hat on the ground.

Belle hurried inside the gloomy castle. "Papa? Are you here? It's Belle." No one replied. Belle didn't know it, but the enchanted objects had seen her. Lumiere danced excitedly around Cogsworth.

"Don't you see? She's the one! She has come to break the spell!"

Finally, Belle discovered Maurice locked in a tower. "Papa!" she said. "We have to get you out of there!"

Suddenly, Belle heard a voice from the shadows.

"What're you doing here?" asked the voice. Belle gasped.

"Please let my father go," she begged. "Take me instead!"

Belle asked the voice to step into the light. She was horrified when she saw the huge, ugly Beast. But to save her father, she agreed to stay in the Beast's castle forever.

The Beast threw Maurice into a carriage that would return him to the village. There, the inventor stumbled into a tavern where Gaston was surrounded by his friends. "Please, I need your help!" he said.

"A horrible beast has Belle locked in a dungeon!"

Gaston and his pals laughed at Maurice, and tossed him out of the tavern. But Maurice's wild story gave Gaston an idea.

At the castle, Belle nervously followed the Beast upstairs, to her room.
"The castle is your home now," he said. "You can go anywhere you
like ... except the West Wing." "What's in the West Wing?" asked Belle.

"It's forbidden!" the Beast shouted. "You will join me for dinner–
that's not a request!" After the Beast stomped off, Belle flung herself
on the bed.

"I'll never escape from this prison, or see my father again!" she said.

That night, Belle refused to dine with the Beast. Later in the evening, she crept downstairs to the kitchen. All the enchanted objects fed and entertained her. Then Cogsworth agreed to take her on a tour.

Belle halted beneath a darkened staircase. "What's up there?" she asked. "Nothing, absolutely nothing of interest at all in the West Wing," Cogsworth replied. But when Cogsworth wasn't looking, Belle slipped away and raced up the staircase to a long hallway lined with broken mirrors.

At the end of the hallway Belle entered a dank, filthy room. The only beautiful object in the room was a rose, shimmering beneath a glass dome.

Entranced, Belle lifted the cover and reached out to touch one soft, pink petal. She did not hear the Beast enter the room.

"I warned you never to come here!" the Beast yelled, advancing on Belle. "GET OUT! GET OUT!"

Terrified by his rage, she turned and ran.

Belle rushed past Cogsworth and Lumiere, as she fled the castle.
She found Phillipe and they galloped through the snow until they
met a pack of fierce, hungry wolves. Terrified, the horse reared and
Belle fell to the ground. When Belle tried to defend Phillipe, the
wolves turned on her, snarling.

Suddenly, a large paw scared the animals off. It was the Beast!

The fierce wolves attacked the Beast, but with a ferocious howl, he fought them off. As the wolves ran off, the Beast collapsed, wounded. Belle knew that this was her chance to escape, but she could not leave the fallen Beast. "Here, I will help you back to the castle," she said.

Meanwhile, Gaston and Le Fou were plotting to have Maurice put in Monsieur D'Arque's insane asylum, unless Belle agreed to marry Gaston.

At the castle, Belle cleaned the Beast's wounds and thanked him
for saving her life. Later, she was quite surprised when he showed her
a beautiful library. "I can't believe it! I've never seen so many books
in all my life!" she gasped.

The Beast smiled for the first time. "Then it's yours," he said.

"Oh, thank you so much!" said a grateful Belle.

Gradually, the mood in the castle began to change. Belle and the Beast read together, dined together, and played together in the snow.

When Belle watched the Beast try to feed some birds, she realized that he had a kind, gentle side to him. In turn, the Beast began to hope that Belle would begin to care for him. He tidied his room, bathed, and dressed up for the evening. He was overjoyed when Belle taught him how to dance.

One evening, the Beast asked Belle if she was happy. "Yes," she replied.

"I only wish I could see my father." The Beast showed Belle the magic mirror. In it, she saw her father lost in the woods. When the Beast saw how worried Belle was, he decided to let her go. Before she left, he gave her the magic mirror. "Take it with you, so you'll always have a way to look back and remember me," he said.

When Belle found her poor father in the forest, she brought him home to their cottage. But almost as soon as they arrived, Monsieur D'Arque knocked on the door. He had come to take her father to an insane asylum!

"No! I won't let you!" cried Belle, as the villagers looked on.

Le Fou had convinced the villagers that Maurice was crazy, because he was raving like a lunatic about some terrible beast.

"I can clear up this little misunderstanding–if you marry me," said Gaston.

"I'll never marry you!" Belle cried. "My father's not crazy. I can prove it!"

Belle showed them the Beast in the magic mirror. "He's not vicious. He's really kind and gentle." Enraged, Gaston shouted, "She's as crazy as the old man! I say we kill the Beast!"

The mob of villagers locked Belle and her father in the cellar and stormed the Beast's castle.

As the villagers battled the enchanted objects, Gaston forced the Beast onto the castle roof. He clubbed the Beast who didn't even try to resist.

"Stop!" yelled Belle. Chip had helped Belle and Maurice escape from the cellar. When the Beast saw Belle, he grabbed Gaston by the throat. But his love for Belle had made him too human. He let Gaston go and faced Belle. Without warning, Gaston stabbed the Beast in the back! The Beast roared. Gaston stepped back–and tumbled off the roof to his death.

Wounded, the Beast gazed up at Belle before he collapsed. She ran to him and held him in her arms. "No! Please! I love you!" she cried.

Suddenly, the rain began to shimmer. Slowly, the Beast transformed into a handsome Prince. "Belle, it's me!" he said.

Belle hesitated and looked into his eyes. "It is you!" she said.

The Prince drew her close and kissed her.

Then they watched happily as Cogsworth, Lumiere, Chip, Mrs. Potts and all the other servants became human once again.

True love had finally broken the spell, and Belle and her Prince danced for joy.

Once upon a time, a little mermaid named Ariel frolicked below the ocean, exploring the hulls of sunken ships with her roly-poly playmate, Flounder.

Swimming inside a ship's cabin, Ariel discovered some rusted silverware. "Oh, my gosh! Have you ever seen anything so wonderful?" she asked the nervous Flounder.

Ariel swam to the water's surface and found her seagull friend.
"Scuttle, look what we've found!" she said, holding up the fork.
"It's a dinglehopper," Scuttle explained. "Humans use these to
straighten their hair."

"Thanks Scuttle!" said Ariel. "It's perfect for my collection."

Ariel dived to an undersea grotto, where she kept her treasures
from the human world. She hid her collection there because her
father, King Triton, forbade merpeople to have any contact
with humans.

That night, Ariel saw strange lights shimmering over the ocean and swam up to investigate. She watched as fireworks flared above a large sailing ship. Scuttle soared down through the flickering colors.

"Some celebration, huh, sweetie? It's the birthday of the human they call Prince Eric."

Ariel peered at the young man on deck. "I've never seen a human this close. He's very handsome."

Aboard the ship, Eric's advisor, Sir Grimsby, motioned for the crew's attention. "It is now my privilege to present our esteemed Prince with a very expensive, very large birthday gift."

He pointed to a marble statue, carved in the Prince's exact likeness!

"Of course, I had hoped it would be a wedding present."

"Don't start, Grim," said the Prince. "The right girl's out there … somewhere."

Far beneath the ocean, the wicked Sea Witch, Ursula, used her magic to spy on Ariel. "My, my ... the daughter of the great Sea King, Triton, in love with a human! A prince, no less. Her daddy will love that! Serves him right, that miserable old tyrant!

Banishing me from his palace, just because I was a little ambitious. Still, this headstrong, lovesick girl may be the key to my revenge on Triton."

On the surface, a sudden storm whipped across the ocean.
The Prince took charge. "Stand fast! Secure the rigging!"
Suddenly, a huge bolt of lightning struck the vessel.
Sir Grimsby slid across the deck. "Eric, look out! The mast is
falling!" Ariel watched in horror. "Eric's been knocked into the
water! I've got to save him!" she cried.

With the storm swirling about her, Ariel desperately searched for
Eric. Diving beneath the huge waves, she spotted the unconscious
Prince. She took hold of him and, using all her strength, managed to
drag him to the surface.

As the storm died down, Ariel dragged the unconscious Prince
to shore. "He's still breathing!" she cried.

Ariel wished that she could stay with the handsome Prince Eric.

She sang a haunting melody that voiced her longing to be with
him forever.

A moment later, Ariel was back in the water, and Sir Grimsby was kneeling beside Eric. "You really delight in these sadistic strains on my blood pressure, don't you?" Sir Grimsby said.

"A girl rescued me," replied Eric. "She had the most beautiful voice …" "I think you've swallowed a bit too much seawater!" said Sir Grimsby, leading Eric away.

Back at the sea king's palace, Triton noticed Ariel floating about, as if in a dream. Summoning Sebastian the crab, the sea king smiled. "You've been keeping something from me. I can tell Ariel's in love."

"I tried to stop her! I told her to stay away from humans!" said Sebastian.

"Humans! Ariel is in love with a human?" asked King Triton, growing angry. Triton found Ariel in her grotto. She was staring at Eric's statue, which Flounder had retrieved after the storm.

"How many times have I told you to stay away from those fish-eating barbarians! Humans are dangerous!" her father shouted.

"But, Daddy, I love him!" said Ariel.

"So help me, Ariel, I am going to get through to you no matter what it takes!" said King Triton. Raising his trident, the sea king destroyed all her treasures. Then he stormed off, leaving Ariel in tears.

As Ariel wept, two eels slithered up to her. "Don't be scared … we represent someone who can help you!"

Ariel followed them to Ursula's den. "My dear, sweet child," Ursula began. "I help poor unfortunate merpeople like yourself. I'll make a potion that will turn you into a human for three days. Before sunset on the third day, you've got to get the prince to fall in love with you, and kiss you. If he does, you'll be human permanently. But if he doesn't, you'll turn back into a mermaid, and you'll belong to me!"

Ariel took a deep breath and nodded. The sea witch smiled deviously. "Oh yes, I almost forgot. We haven't discussed payment. I'm not asking much. All I want is—your voice!"

Ariel thought of her prince. Then she reluctantly agreed.

Ursula used her powers to capture Ariel's beautiful voice in a seashell, and transform the Little Mermaid into a human!

Aided by Sebastian and Flounder, Ariel used her new legs to swim awkwardly to shore. There she found Prince Eric walking his dog. He studied Ariel as she shied away from the animal.

"You ... you seem very familiar to me. Have we met?" he asked. Ariel opened her mouth to answer, but her voice was gone.

"You can't speak?" asked the prince, lowering his eyes. "Then I guess we haven't met."

Eric guessed that Ariel had been in a shipwreck, so he took her back to the palace. At the palace, Ariel was whisked upstairs by a maid.

Grimsby discovered the prince staring glumly out the window. "Eric, be reasonable! Young ladies don't swim around rescuing people!" "I'm telling you, she was real!" said the Prince. "I'm going to find her!"

A moment later, Ariel appeared in a beautiful gown …

The following afternoon, Eric took Ariel for a rowboat ride across a lagoon. Sebastian swam nearby. Almost two days had gone by and the prince hadn't kissed Ariel! Sebastian decided to create a romantic mood. He began conducting a chorus of sea creatures, and the music worked! Eric leaned over to kiss Ariel. But as he bent toward her, the boat tipped, and both Eric and Ariel fell into the water!

From her ocean lair, Ursula saw them tumble into the lagoon. "That was a close one! I can't let Ariel get away that easily!"

She began concocting a magic potion. "Soon Triton's daughter will be mine! Then I'll make the sea king writhe and wriggle like a worm on a hook!"

The next morning, Scuttle told Ariel that the prince had announced his wedding! Overjoyed, Ariel hurried downstairs. But she hid when she saw Eric introducing Grimsby to a mysterious, dark-haired maiden. The prince seemed hypnotized. "Vanessa saved my life," Eric explained.

"We're going to be married on board ship, at sunset."

Ariel drew back, confused. She was the one who had rescued Eric!

Sebastian and Flounder found Ariel sitting on the dock, watching the wedding ship leave the harbor. Suddenly, Scuttle crash-landed beside them.

"I flew over the ship and saw Vanessa's reflection in a mirror. She's the sea witch, in disguise! And she's wearing the seashell containing Ariel's voice. We've got to stop the wedding!"

Flounder helped Ariel swim out to the boat, while Sebastian went to get the sea king.

Dripping wet, Ariel climbed aboard the ship just before sunset, as Eric and the maiden were about to be married.

Before Vanessa could say "I do," Scuttle and an army of his friends attacked her.

In the scuffle, Vanessa's seashell necklace crashed to the deck,
freeing Ariel's voice. Suddenly, Vanessa sounded like the sea witch.
"Eric, get away from her!" she cried.
Ariel smiled at the prince. "Oh Eric, I wanted to tell you …"
Ursula grinned. "You're too late! The sun has set!"
Ariel felt her body changing back into a mermaid.

"Poor little princess," said Ursula, dragging Ariel into the water.
"It's not you I'm after. You're merely the bait to catch your father."
"Ursula, stop!" shouted a furious King Triton, swimming towards
them. "I'll make a deal with you—just don't harm my daughter!"
Instantly, Triton was changed into a tiny plant.
Ariel stood heartbroken before Ursula, now Queen of the Ocean.

Suddenly, Prince Eric appeared. He tossed a harpoon at the sea witch, hitting her in the arm.

"You little fool!" Ursula yelled, snatching up the King's trident.

As the sea witch pointed the weapon at Eric, Ariel rammed into her, knocking the trident loose.

"Eric, we have to get away from here!" she cried. The moment Ariel and Eric surfaced from the water, huge tentacles shot out of the ocean.

An enormous monster emerged–it was the sea witch! Ursula commanded the waters into a deadly whirlpool, and several old sunken ships rose to the surface.

Eric struggled aboard one of the ships. Then he steered the ship right into the sea witch, destroying her. The mighty force sent Eric reeling toward shore.

As the unconscious prince lay on the beach, Ariel perched on a rock and gazed at him. Triton had returned to normal after Ursula had been destroyed. He and Sebastian watched, from afar. The sea king saw that his daughter really did love the prince. He waved his trident, and Ariel was once again human.

The next day, Ariel and Prince Eric were married. As they kissed, the humans and merpeople sent up a happy cheer, linked at last by the marriage of two people whose love was as deep as the sea and as pure as a young girl's voice.

inderella

WALT DISNEY'S
Cinderella

Once upon a time, in a tiny kingdom, there was a gentle and lovely girl named Cinderella. She lived with her cruel stepmother and two wicked stepsisters.

They were jealous of Cinderella's goodness and beauty, and made her work night and day. The mice and the birds were Cinderella's only friends.

Cinderella did all the cooking, scrubbing, washing and mending, while her selfish stepsisters did nothing. But Cinderella never complained. She believed that someday, her dreams of happiness would come true.

One day, an invitation arrived from the King. That night, a royal ball was to be held in honor of the Prince. Every young maiden in the kingdom was commanded to attend.

Cinderella was very excited. "That means I can go, too!"
Her stepsisters just laughed.

"But the announcement said every maiden was to attend,"
said Cinderella.

"Very well, Cinderella, you can go–after you finish all your chores," said her stepmother. "Now wash this slip for me. Mend these buttonholes.

Where's my sash? Press this dress. Curl my hair. Oh, and find my fan!"

Cinderella's stepmother kept her busy all day long.

Soon it was time to leave, but Cinderella had not had time to fix her one and only old ball gown.

Sadly, she decided not to go to the ball.

But … Cinderella's little animal friends had a surprise for her. They had fixed her old gown, and it was beautiful!

Cinderella was so happy. Now she could go to the ball, after all!
But when Cinderella's wicked stepsisters saw how beautiful she
looked, they were furious. In a rage, they tore the gown to pieces.
Then they left for the ball with their mother.

Poor Cinderella burst into tears, and ran into the garden.

"I thought someday my dreams would come true," she sobbed.
"Now I'll never get to the royal ball."

"Yes, you will, child, but we must hurry," said a kind voice.
Cinderella looked up, and there sat her Fairy Godmother.

"Let's see, now," said the Fairy Godmother. "I'll need a pumpkin and some mice." Then she waved her magic wand and said some magic words. To Cinderella's amazement, the pumpkin became a splendid coach, and the mice turned into elegant horses!

"Oh, this is wonderful," cried Cinderella. But then she looked down at her ragged clothes. "Don't you think my dress …"

"Lovely, my dear," began the Fairy Godmother. Then she looked again. "Oh, good heavens, child! You can't go in that!"

She waved her magic wand again and there stood Cinderella, in the loveliest gown she had ever seen. On her tiny feet were delicate glass slippers.

Cinderella was delighted. "Oh, Fairy Godmother–it's like a dream come true!"

"Yes, child. But like all dreams, it can't last forever. On the stroke of midnight, the spell will be broken, and everything will be as it was before."

"I'll remember," promised Cinderella. "Oh, it's more than I ever hoped for!"

"Bless you, my child," said the Fairy Godmother. Cinderella stepped into the pumpkin coach and was whisked away to the royal ball.

The King's ballroom was magnificent. Every lady in the land was dressed in her finest gown. But Cinderella was the loveliest of them all.

When the Prince saw the charming Cinderella, he fell in love instantly.

The Grand Duke said to the King, "You see, Your Majesty, the Prince has danced with that girl all evening. It looks like he's found the girl he wants to marry."

But soon, the tower clock began to strike midnight.
Cinderella cried, "Oh, I almost forgot!" And without another
word, away she ran, out of the ballroom and down the palace stairs.
On the way, she lost one of her glass slippers, but she couldn't stop
to get it.

Cinderella stepped into the magic coach, and quickly rode away.
As the clock struck for the twelfth time, the magic ended!

Cinderella was left with a pumpkin, some mice, and the wonderful memory of her magical evening.

The next morning, the whole kingdom was wondering who the-mysterious girl was. The only clue was the lost slipper.

The Grand Duke carried the glass slipper from house to house, looking for its owner, for the Prince said he would marry no one but the girl who could wear the tiny slipper.

Every girl in the land tried hard to put the slipper on. The wicked stepsisters tried hardest of all! But it was no use. Not a single girl could fit her foot into the tiny glass shoe.

And where was Cinderella? Locked in her room! Her mean old stepmother was taking no chances that poor Cinderella would try on the slipper.

But Cinderella's mice friends found the key, and rushed it up to the locked room.

The Duke was just about to leave. "Well, madam, if you have no other daughters, I'll bid you good day."

Just then, he heard a voice calling to him.

"Please wait! May I try the slipper?" It was Cinderella.

"Of course," said the Duke. "Every girl must have a chance. Please sit down."

He slid the glass slipper onto Cinderella's foot, and it fit perfectly.

Cinderella's dreams had come true. No longer would she work for her cruel stepmother and her foolish stepsisters. She would marry the handsome Prince.

And what became of the little mice and birds, who had been Cinderella's only friends? They went to the palace, too.

And they all lived happily ever after.

Snow White

WALT DISNEY's

Snow White
and the Seven Dwarfs

Once upon a time, there lived a lovely princess named
Snow White.

Her vain and wicked stepmother, the Queen, feared that one day
Snow White's beauty would surpass her own. So she dressed the
princess in rags, and forced her to work as a servant in the castle.

Each day, the Queen consulted her Magic Mirror.

"Magic Mirror on the wall, who is the fairest one of all?"

As long as the mirror responded in the Queen's favor, Snow White
was safe.

One day, as Snow White was drawing water from a well, she made a wish. She wished that the one she loved would find her.

As she gazed into the wishing well, she saw another face reflected in the water. It belonged to a handsome prince.

"Hello. Did I frighten you? Please don't run away!" said the Prince.

But the startled princess had fled to her balcony.

The Queen was spying on Snow White and the Prince. She flew into a jealous rage and rushed to her Magic Mirror, demanding an answer.

"Famed is thy beauty, Majesty, but hold! A lovely maid I see. Rags cannot hide her gentle grace. She is more fair than thee," said the mirror. "Alas for her! Reveal her name," said the Queen.

"Lips red as a rose, hair black as ebony, skin white as snow…" was the reply. The Queen gasped. "SNOW WHITE!"

Furious, the Queen sent for her Huntsman. "Take Snow White far into the forest. Find some secluded glade where she can pick wildflowers. And there, my faithful Huntsman, you will kill her!"

"But your Majesty, the little Princess–," he said.

"Silence! You know the penalty if you fail," the Queen replied.

Knowing that he dare not disobey the Queen, the Huntsman led Snow White into the forest. But when it came time for him to harm Snow White, he stopped and fell to his knees.

"I can't do it. Forgive me, Your Highness!" he said.

"Why, why—I don't understand," Snow White replied.

"The Queen is mad! She's jealous of you. She'll stop at nothing. Now quick, child—run, run away. Hide in the woods! Anywhere! And never come back!" cried the Huntsman.

Frightened and alone, Snow White ran into the forest.
Blazing eyes peered out at her from the darkness.
Eerie shrieks pierced the air. Tree branches grabbed at her.

Finally she could run no further, and fell to the ground, sobbing. When Snow White looked up, she saw several forest animals gathered around her.

"Hello," she said. "Do you know where I can stay? Maybe in the woods somewhere?"

Snow White followed the animals to a little cottage in the woods. She knocked on the door, but no one answered. So she went inside.

"Oh, it's adorable! Just like a doll's house," she said. "Why, there are seven little chairs. There must be seven little children. And by the look of this table, seven untidy children. I know—I'll clean house and surprise them. Then maybe they'll let me stay."

With the help of her animal friends, Snow White cleaned the cottage. Then she decided to check upstairs.

"What adorable little beds. And look—they have names carved on them. Doc, Happy, Sneezy, Dopey—what funny names for children! And there's Grumpy, Bashful, and Sleepy. I'm a little sleepy myself." Snow White laid down across three of the tiny beds and fell asleep.

Just then, the owners of the cottage came marching home.
They weren't children at all, but the Seven Dwarfs, who worked all day in their diamond mine.

As they marched into the clearing, the Dwarfs came to a halt.
"Look–our house! The lit's light … the light's lit," said Doc.
"Mark my words, there's trouble a-brewin'," said Grumpy.
"I felt it comin' on all day."
The Dwarfs peeked inside the cottage and saw that the whole place was clean!

Suddenly, the Dwarfs thought they heard a sound. Doc looked towards the stairs. "I-i-it's up there. In the bedroom."

Cautiously, the seven little men went in to investigate. They slowly opened the door and peered in. "Why, i-i-it's a girl," said Doc.

As the Dwarfs approached the sleeping Princess, she began to stir. They quickly hid behind the beds.

Snow White yawned and stretched. Then she noticed seven pairs of eyes looking at her, over the end of the beds. She sat up, smiling.

"How do you do?" she said.

"How do you do what?" Grumpy folded his arms, scowling.

Snow White laughed. "Let me guess. You must be Grumpy."

"Heh! I know who I am. Who are you?"

"Oh, how silly of me. I'm Snow White."

"The princess?" Doc looked very impressed.

"Tell her to go back where she belongs," said Grumpy.

"Please don't send me away!" pleaded Snow White. "If you do, the Queen will kill me!"

Grumpy shook his head. "The Queen's an old witch. If she finds you here, she'll swoop down and wreak her vengeance on us!"

"Oh, she'll never find me here," said Snow White. "And if you let me stay, I'll keep house for you. I'll wash and sew and sweep and cook..." "Cook!" Doc rubbed his tummy. "Hooray! She stays!"

Back in the castle, the wicked Queen stood before her mirror. "Magic Mirror on the wall, who now is the fairest one of all?"

"Beyond the seventh fall, in the cottage of the Seven Dwarfs, Snow White still lives, fairest one of all."

"I've been tricked!" yelled the Queen. "I'll go myself, to the Dwarfs' cottage in the woods. I'll go in disguise so complete, no one will suspect me."

The Queen concocted a magic potion, then transformed herself into an ugly old peddler woman.

"And now, a special sort of death for one so fair. What should it be?"

"Ah, a poisoned apple! One taste and Snow White's eyes will close forever, only to be revived by love's first kiss. No fear of that! The Dwarfs will think she's dead!"

Back at the cottage, Snow White kissed each of the Dwarfs goodbye as they set off for work.

"Now don't forget, my dear, the old Queen's a sly one. Full of witchcraft, so beware," said Doc.

Then Grumpy frowned. "Now, I'm warnin' ya, don't let nobody or nothin' in the house."

Snow White smiled at him. "Why, Grumpy, you do care!"

Shortly after the Dwarfs left, the old peddler woman appeared at the cottage. She asked Snow White if she was making pies.

"Yes, gooseberry pies," replied Snow White.

"Ahh, it's apple pies that make the menfolks' mouths water. Pies made with apples like these," said the old woman.

She took a shiny red apple from her basket and offered it to Snow White.

Sensing that Snow White was in danger, several birds swooped down on the woman, knocking the apple out of her hand.

Snow White tried to shoo the birds away. "Stop it!" she cried. "Go away! Shame on you, frightening the poor old lady."

"Oh, my heart. Oh, my. My poor heart. Take me into the house and let me rest. A drink of water, please," said the peddler woman.

Unable to make Snow White understand, the birds and animals raced to alert the Dwarfs. At the mine, they pulled and tugged at the men. "What ails these crazy critters?" Grumpy growled.

Doc thought about it. "Maybe it's the Queen!"

Grumpy galloped off on the back of a deer. "Snow White's in danger! We've gotta save her."

Meanwhile, the Queen was tempting Snow White with the poisoned apple. "Because you've been so good to poor old granny, I'll share a secret with you. This is no ordinary apple. It's a magic wishing apple!"

"A wishing apple, really?" asked Snow White.

"Yes. One bite and all your dreams will come true," said the Queen.

The old woman grinned at Snow White. "Perhaps there's someone you love?" she asked.

"Well, there is someone," the Princess replied.

"I thought so. Old Granny knows a young girl's heart. Now make a wish and take a bite."

Snow White did so. "Oh, I feel strange," she said. A moment later, she fell to the ground.

A storm began to rage as the Dwarfs reached the cottage, and found the lifeless Snow White. Grumpy spotted the old hag disappearing into the forest. "There she goes, men. After her!"

The Dwarfs chased the Queen up a steep cliff. "You little fools, I'll crush yer bones!" she cried, trying to pry a boulder loose, to crush them. Suddenly, a bolt of lightning shattered the ledge, sending the wicked Queen into the valley below.

Though the evil Queen was gone forever, the princess was still locked in her spell. So beautiful was she, even in death, that the Dwarfs could not find it in their hearts to bury her.

Doc brushed away a tear. "Let's make her a casket out of crystal and gold. That way we can still see her, and keep constant watch by her side."

The Prince heard of the beautiful maiden who slept in the crystal casket. He rode to the cottage of the Seven Dwarfs, and they took him to Snow White. Gently, he kissed her. Then, slowly, her eyes began to open. The spell was broken. Love's first kiss had brought her back to life!

Snow White's wish finally came true. She bid the Seven Dwarfs goodbye as the handsome Prince swept her into his arms.

Soon wedding bells rang, echoing throughout the forest.

From then on, Snow White and her prince lived in their castle happily ever after …